CLIFFORD'S BEST SCHOOL DAY

by Quinlan B. Lee

Illustrated by Steve Haefele

Based on the Scholastic book series
"Clifford The Big Red Dog"
by Norman Bridwell

No part of this publication may be reproduced in whole or in part, stored in a retrieval system, or transmitted in any form or by any means, electronic, mechanical, photocopying, recording, or otherwise, without written permission of the publisher. For information regarding permission, write to Scholastic Inc., Attention: Permissions Department, 557 Broadway, New York, NY 10012.

ISBN-13: 978-0-545-02844-8
ISBN-10: 0-545-02844-2

Designed by Michael Massen

12 11 10 9 8 7 6   12 13 14 15/0

Printed in the U.S.A.   40
First printing, September 2007

"I'm home!" called Emily Elizabeth.

Clifford was happy.

Woof!

"Did you have a good day at school?"

asked Mom.

"How was your test?"

Emily Elizabeth smiled. "A plus."

"Way to go!" said Mom.

"I know just the spot for it."

"Look at that board," said Cleo.

"Emily Elizabeth is good at so many things."

T-Bone whistled. "You must

be really proud."

"I am," said Clifford.

Clifford looked at all the awards.

"I want Emily Elizabeth to be proud of me, too," he said.

"Okay, big guy," said Cleo.

"So what are you really good at doing?"

"I can dig holes," said Clifford. "Really big ones!"

"Do it!" cheered T-Bone.

Clifford dug the biggest, best hole ever.

"Uh-oh," said Cleo. "Maybe biggest
isn't the best.
What else can you do?"

"I can fetch balls," said Clifford.

"Really high ones!"

Clifford ran to fetch Emily Elizabeth's ball.

"Oh, no," cried Emily Elizabeth.

"That's not your ball, Clifford."

"Game over," Charley said.

The next day, Emily Elizabeth looked
as down as Clifford when she got home.
"What's wrong?" Mom asked.
"Bad day at school?"

"I can't decide what to draw for the great big
art show at school tomorrow."

Mom smiled. "I think you're forgetting the biggest, greatest thing we know."

"Clifford!" cried Emily Elizabeth.

Woof!

Emily Elizabeth couldn't wait to go to school the next day.

Clifford had a great time posing for art class.

And then came the best thing of all.

Emily Elizabeth won first place in the
art show!

When they got home, Emily Elizabeth hung the blue ribbon on Clifford's doghouse. "I couldn't have done it without you, Clifford," she said.

"Emily Elizabeth," Mom called. "Time to start your homework."

"Okay, Mom," she said. "Want to help, Clifford?"

"I have to write about someone I'm proud of, and I know exactly who it will be!"

Do You Remember?

Circle the right answer.

1. Why did Clifford dig a big hole?
   a. Because Cleo told him to do it.
   b. To hide a big bone.
   c. He wanted Emily Elizabeth to be proud of him.

2. What did Emily Elizabeth hang on Clifford's doghouse?
   a. A blue ribbon.
   b. A drawing of Clifford.
   c. A big sign.

Which happened first?

Which happened next?

Which happened last?

Write a 1, 2, or 3 in the space after each sentence.

Emily Elizabeth won first place in the art show. _____

Clifford fetched Emily Elizabeth's basketball. _____

Clifford went to school. _____

Answers:

1. c
2. a
Emily Elizabeth won first place in the art show. (3)
Clifford fetched Emily Elizabeth's basketball. (1)
Clifford went to school. (2)